BOOK #4

OTTO UNDERCOVER

★ TOXIC TAFFY TAKEOVER ★

RHEA PERLMAN

ILLUSTRATED BY

DAN SANTAT

KATHERINE TEGEN BOOKS

An Imprint of HarperCollinsPublishers

For these great kids:

Zachary Kurland, Jessie and Maya Miller,
Anthony and Joey DeVito

Thanks to all the kids in Ms. Simmerman's fourth-grade
class and Mrs. Held's fifth-grade class at the Aragon
School in Los Angeles and Ian (Mufasa) Harrington.

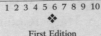

Otto Undercover #4: Toxic Taffy Takeover

Text copyright © 2006 by Rhea Perlman

Illustrations copyright © 2006 by Dan Santat

Library of Congress Cataloging-in-Publication Data is available.

ISBN-10: 0-06-075501-6 (pbk.) —ISBN-13: 978-0-06-075501-0 (pbk.)
ISBN 10: 0-06-075502-4 (trade bdg.)—ISBN-13: 978-0-06-075502-7 (trade bdg.)

1 2 3 4 5 6 7 8 9 10
❖
First Edition

CONTENTS

AUNT FOOFOO AKA AUNT OOFOOF

Alias: Uncle FroFro AKA Uncle OrfOrf
Occupations:
- Assistant Secret Agent
- Pit Crew Co-Chief

Hobby: World-Famous Chef

AUNT FIFI AKA AUNT IFIF

Alias: Uncle FriFri AKA Uncle IrfIrf
Occupations:
- Assistant Secret Agent
- Pit Crew Co-Chief

Hobbies: Tap Dancing/Singing
Problem Area: Can Only Sing the Note A-flat

RACECAR

Designer: Otto Pillip
Driver: Otto Pillip
Feature: Fastest Car on Earth
Special Features:

- Claw
- Vacu-Zap
- Voice Command
- A Million More Things

Extra-Special Feature: Can Morph into Other Vehicles

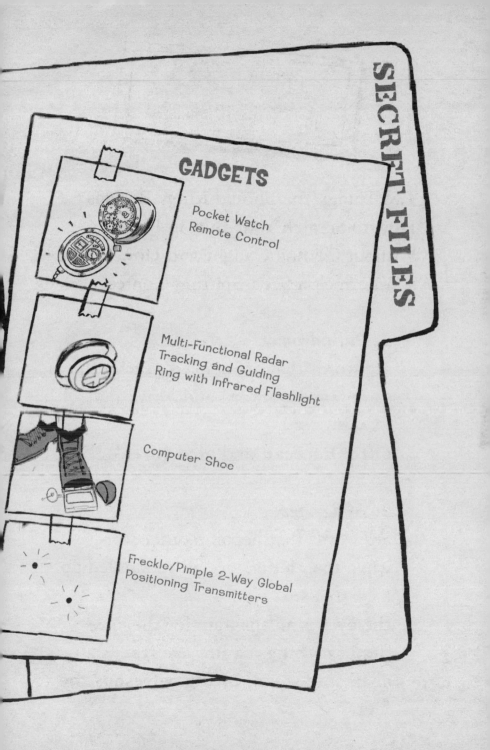

GADGETS

Pocket Watch
Remote Control

Multi-Functional Radar
Tracking and Guiding
Ring with Infrared Flashlight

Computer Shoe

Freckle/Pimple 2-Way Global
Positioning Transmitters

USELESS INFORMATION

Two Things You Should Know Besides How to Scratch Your Butt in Public Without Getting Caught and How to Win a Watermelon Seed-Spitting Contest

1. Palindromes

are words that are spelled exactly the same way backward and forward.

EXAMPLES:

Otto, Racecar, and **bird rib.**

2. Anagrams

are words that become other words when their letters are all scrambled up.

EXAMPLES:

the eyes is an anagram for **they see**

the best things in life are free is an anagram for **nail biting refreshes the feet**

The End of Book Three

It was Sunday night and Otto had just completed his third mission. He had gotten rid of the lunatic, Pruneman, and found out that his parents were being chased by a tall skinny man with an enormous neck and a long dangling head.

He was in the garage, standing on his amplifier, wearing his antenna hat, chewing an orange gum ball, playing the guitar, singing "The Dried Fruit Blues" in the note of G.

Then a million things happened at once.

CHAPTER 1

Smoke and Bubbles

Otto's antenna hat started buzzing, the gum in his mouth started growing, his eye started pulsing, and he heard a rustling noise outside the garage window.

A bubble the size of Otto's face popped out of his mouth. Wispy smoke swirled inside it, creating letters that formed into an anagram. It was a message from the agency he worked for, Eee YiiiY Eee.

This one said:

WIRY NECK
TOY ON
Tight

Then there was a loud crash as the garage window broke, and a long leg started feeling its way into the room.

CHAPTER 2

No Time for Numskulls

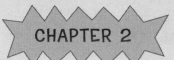

Otto jumped onto the leg and yelled for backup.

Aunt FooFoo came out of nowhere and pounced. There was a loud howl from the other side of the window. Aunt FiFi bounded into the room and gnawed at the leg with her fearsome false teeth.

"Hold on to him," cried Otto. "It may be the tall skinny man with the long dangling head."

They pulled hard. Too hard. The intruder's pant legs tore off.

"He's getting away," yelled Otto.

The intruder yelled back as he ran limping down the street, "I'm gonna get you for this, Blotto."

"Oh fooey! It's just that lousy loser sneak, Wilson Carlson Fullsom," said Otto.

Fullsom was a racecar driver and a big creep. He hated Otto's guts because Otto won every race. Earlier that day, Otto had been called on a mission and left the Fleabag 500 auto race before it had even begun. This was Fullsom's big chance, but he had been disqualified for hopping around the track like a chicken.

"Let's go after him and pound his flabby flesh to a pulp," said FiFi, who was about the size of Fullsom's rib cage.

"We don't have time for that numskull now," said Otto. "My parents or someone else at Eee YiiiY Eee sent us our next mission. Check it out."

Otto blew another bubble. The smoky letters inside it started circling. Otto adjusted the antenna on his hat. This time the letters formed the words:

"We've got to get to the airport," said Otto. He zoomed up to his loft and threw a couple of things into a backpack.

"What are you waiting for," he said to The Aunts. They stood there staring at him. "Put on your Uncle disguises, and let's go."

"But we just got back from the water balloon thing. What about sleeping?" asked FiFi.

"What's today?" asked Otto.

"Sunday," said FiFi.

"Sunday?" said Otto. "We just slept last night."

"Yes, I remember that," sighed Aunt FooFoo. "It was so warm and cozy, with blankets and pillows and everything. I'd love to do it again sometime."

The Aunts went into their phone booth and changed into their Uncle disguises.

Then they all piled into Racecar and took off.

CHAPTER 3

Option 16

"What about the car? Huh, Otto, what are you going to do about that?" asked FiFi. "You can't take it on the plane, you know."

"That's true, Ottie," said FooFoo. "According to the Federal Association of Airplanes, all cars must be in a car carrier and tranquilized. And then they have to go in the baggage compartment with the suitcases and other items."

"That's pets," said Otto, "and I think you forgot about *Option 16*."

They arrived at the airport.

Otto ejected his shoe computer. He used the tips of his shoelace to press *Option 16* on

the screen. Racecar started to bubble and turn to jelly. He shrunk smaller and smaller until he was just a metal charm in the shape of a car.

"Here it is: Racecar Concentrate," said Otto. He hung the charm on a leather

string and tied it around his neck.

"Okay, let's go."

CHAPTER 4

Hardly Moving

Otto's second clue was in the magazine he found in the airplane seat pocket. It was a picture of the Coney Island section of Brooklyn, New York. Coney Island is not a regular island like Hawaii or anything, but a city neighborhood with lots of rides and attractions.

In the magazine was a double-page spread featuring the boardwalk, the Cyclone roller coaster, the Wonder Wheel, and the Parachute Jump. There were ads for cotton candy, caramel apples, and soft ice cream swirls. It looked like a great place.

As Otto stared at the pages, he realized they contained a message.

That's the most ridiculous anagram yet, thought Otto. It was a tough one too. There were too many combinations, but at least he had something to keep him busy on the long flight. At 700 miles per hour, Otto felt like the plane was crawling. He made a mental note to work on a flying machine that could actually get somewhere fast.

By the time they touched down, Otto had figured out the anagram. They were going to Coney Island, and they had to be pretty careful about what they ate when they got there.

CHAPTER 5

Three O'clock in the Morning

Otto and The Uncles rushed through the airport and out into the rainy night outside.

"Get that taxi," said Otto to The Uncles. He dropped the Racecar Concentrate charm into a solution of fizzy water and yeast. It began to grow.

"What taxi?" asked FooFoo.

"This one," said Otto. He tapped *Option 8* on his shoe computer. Racecar morphed into a New York City yellow cab.

Just a few speedy minutes later they were in Coney Island.

The first thing they saw when they got there was a tiny toddler crawling across the dark street all by himself. He

looked like he was only about two years old. Otto slammed on the brakes. He and The Uncles got out.

"Are you okay, little guy?" he asked.

"Daddy!" said the little boy, and he leaped into Otto's arms.

CHAPTER 6

Family Secrets

"I didn't know you had a child," said Aunt FooFoo. She sounded hurt. "You could have told us. We didn't even know you were married."

"I'm not married, Uncle OrfOrf, and this is not my child," said Otto. "I'm just a kid."

"You *L'il* Daddy," said the tiny toddler. "Big Daddy broken." He was wearing a diaper and a jacket with a hood. Under the hood he had another diaper on his head. He was climbing all over Otto.

"Poor little guy, he must be lost or his parents have been hurt. We have to try to find them," said Otto.

"Okay," said FooFoo, "but if he's up for grabs, can I have him? I think he's cute, like a monkey."

The baby boy was hanging on to Otto's hair.

Otto pried the boy's hands off. "What's your name?" he asked.

"L'il Mellem," said the boy, hugging Otto's face and pulling his nose.

A palindrome name, thought Otto, wondering if meeting the little boy was more than just a coincidence.

"Good name," said Aunt FooFoo, thinking the baby had said his name was *L'il* Melon. "He looks a lot like a small cantaloupe."

"TAFFY!" said Aunt FiFi.

"He doesn't look like taffy at all," said Aunt FooFoo. "Maybe a little bit like a gummy bear."

"No, taffy. Look." FiFi pointed to a billboard. On it was a picture of a pile of shimmering taffy. The advertisement said:

It was the kind of sign that flipped around to show another message. On the back it said:

CHAPTER 7

Sweet and Dangerous

"I don't know what **Otooneth Snoone** means," said Otto, "but everyone knows that *live* is an anagram for *evil*."

"Yes, and *vile*," added Aunt FooFoo.

"That's true," said Otto.

"C'mon, let's go get some taffy," said FiFi.

"Listen," said Otto. "When you were sleeping on the plane, I got an anagrammed message that said not to eat any saltwater taffy."

"Oh, well, that was just for you because you're a little chubby. I'm small and adorable and I love taffy," said Aunt FiFi.

"I'm pretty sure the taffy is dangerous, Aunt IfIf, so please don't eat any," said Otto.

"Taffy bad yuck yuck," said *L'il Mellem*.

"See?" said FooFoo.

"What does he know?" said FiFi. "I'm much older than him, and even a little bit bigger."

Glow-in-the-dark arrows pointed the way to the taffy shop.

"C'mon," said Otto. "Let's check it out."

"*Mellem* ride car, rrrrrrm rrrrrrm, chickie poo," said *L'il Mellem*.

"You betcha," said Otto, giggling.

He punched the *Baby Seat* button on the dashboard, and they all piled into Racecar.

CHAPTER 8

Follow the Arrows

CHAPTER 9

Good Weather?

Miss O's Famous Saltwater Taffy Shop was on the boardwalk. Thousands of people milled around out front, even though it was 3:30 in the morning and raining. It

seemed like everyone in Coney Island was there.

They were doing some kind of dance step, picking up one knee and then the other, and flapping their arms. They looked tired and dirty, and their clothes were ragged, but they all had smiles pasted across their faces. They sure seemed happy.

"What's going on here?" asked Otto.

"Beautiful day, isn't it?" replied one man.

"Actually, it's raining," said Otto.

"What should we do now?" asked the man.

"I don't know," said Otto.

"Bright and sunny, I'd say," said another guy.

"I'd say it's night, and it's freezing," said Otto.

"Yup, it's a warm one," said a woman, fanning herself. "What should we do now?"

"There's something wrong with all these people," said Otto. "It's like they're hypnotized or something."

"Don't touch them," said Aunt FooFoo, holding Otto back. "I think they're zombies and they're contagious."

"Who cares about them?" huffed FiFi.

"Where do you get the taffy?" she asked loudly.

Suddenly, every person turned toward the store and began to chant, "Taffy! Taffy!" The noise was deafening.

A loud sound blasted over a speaker system. A very nasal, whiny female voice shouted, "QUIET!"

The door of the shop swung open.

CHAPTER 10

Miss O

A short square woman charged out, holding a megaphone.

The people started chanting, "Miss O! Miss O!"

Miss O wore a long robe, like a queen. It looked like it was made of gold. Layers and layers of sapphire necklaces dangled from her throat. Diamond earrings hung down to her knees, while on her head sat an emerald and ruby baseball cap. She had on so many jewels that for a moment Otto was blinded by their sparkle.

When his eyes focused, he could see that there was something wrong with her face. She had only one tooth, and no nose. Instead, there were two holes where the nostrils should have been, and they were

stuffed with tissues. They seemed to be leaking.

"That's it!" said Otto. "The answer to the anagram! *Otooneth Snoone* unscrambled is *One tooth no nose*."

"Bad lady booger face," said *L'il Mellem*.

Otto quickly hid the baby in his backpack under his jacket.

WARNING

Do not proceed to Chapter 11 until you read this IMPORTANT INFORMATION!!!!!!!!!!!

(The management cannot be responsible for any readers who fail to read the warning and pull their hair out in frustration.)

Otooneth Snoone had a speech impediment. This is because she had no nose. People with no noses have trouble pronouncing some of their letters, especially the letter *S*, which comes out like *TH*. Try it sometime.

(The management cannot be responsible for any readers who cut off their noses to try talking without them.)

Even though ***Otooneth*** had trouble speaking, she was very good at alliteration. This is when you use a series of words that start with the same sound.

(The management cannot be responsible for any readers who drive people crazy saying, "Peter Piper picked a peck of pickled peppers at picnics or parties.")

CHAPTER 11

Otooneth Thpeakth

"Why don't all of you bulbouth, blabbering, birdbrained, bathket cathes leave me alone?!!" whined *Otooneth*.

The chants of "Miss O" and "Taffy, taffy" grew even louder.

"Okay, you dumb doody doofutheth," she said. "What'dya got for me?"

She pranced through the crowd. The first woman took off her only ring, and happily dropped it into *Otooneth*'s pocket. Miss O gave her a piece of twinkling taffy.

The woman ate it greedily.

"Gimme thomething, you ignorant idiot," she said to the next person.

The man emptied out his pockets. All he had was a penny and an old key. "Here you are, Miss O. Warm and sunny, nice and shiny," he said, smiling. She took

them and gave him a piece of taffy.

The next person was a little girl.

"What'dya got, you dithguthting dithrag?" asked Miss O.

The little girl took her only possession, a metal bobby pin, out of her ratty hair. *Otooneth* grabbed it and handed her a piece of taffy.

"Thank you," said the girl happily. "It's just like Christmas."

Otooneth was making her way toward Otto and The Aunts.

"Make believe you're just like the others," said Otto. "Do the knee thing."

Smiling, they jerked their knees up and flapped their arms.

Otooneth got to FooFoo first.

"Gimme thomething, fatty fat fat," *Otooneth* yelled in FooFoo's face, snot dripping down her chin.

FooFoo put her hand in her pocket and took out a tissue. *Otooneth* wiped her nose holes and handed the wet tissue back.

"Ew," said FooFoo.

"What did you thay?" asked *Otooneth* threateningly.

"I said, ew look lovely. What a nice

40

day," said FooFoo.

"Gimme thomething," said **Otooneth**.

FooFoo gave her the cheese sandwich that she happened to have in her other pocket.

"Been holding out on me, eh?" said **Otooneth**, taking the sandwich. She gave FooFoo a piece of taffy and moved on to FiFi.

"What about you, you pygmy pipthqueak?" she said.

FiFi pulled her pockets out. They were empty.

Otooneth turned red. "You get nothing, you nathty newt!" she roared.

"Give me yours," FiFi whispered to FooFoo, and took the taffy out of her hand.

"What do you have,

hideouth humpback?" *Otooneth* yelled at Otto.

Otto quickly pulled 50 cents and a marble out of his pocket. It would be a disaster if *Otooneth* found his pocket watch, or backpack.

"What a lucky lad I am, and happy, too, full of joy, joviality, and jubilation," said Otto.

"You're thtill only getting one piethe of taffy, you lathy lunatic locutht," said *Otooneth* as she moved on.

FiFi unwrapped the taffy and inhaled a wonderful sugary smell. She was about to pop the candy in her mouth when Otto grabbed it out of her hand and put it in his pocket.

"What are you doing? That's poison!" he said.

"Just one piece," said FiFi. "I want it. Taffy. Taffy!"

"Peekaboo, taffy lady cuckoo face," said *L'il Mellem*, peeping out from the backpack.

It was a ***fortunate turn o' fate*** that the noise from the crowd was so loud that ***Otooneth*** didn't hear him.

Fortunate is an anagram for turn o' fate.

She snorted into her megaphone. "I'm through with you revolting, rediculouth rodentsth. It'th too much to take! I need to be richer and you don't have anything left to give me. You jutht keep hanging around! You're driving me crathy. It'th time for your parachute ride! Follow me."

CHAPTER 12

Zombies Doomed

The crowd started moving together in one big crush.

Otto pulled his aunts out of the mob and back to Racecar. They drove onto the beach.

"WHOA!" exclaimed Otto. "What is this?!!"

The sand was covered with stuff. There were televisions, stereos, jewelry, and bags of money. There were hundreds of Game Boys, remote-control cars, dolls, bicycles, Rollerblades, and snowboards. There were trailers, cars, yachts, and even an army tank.

Otto looked over at the rides through the binoculars on his ring. The cages of the Wonder Wheel were stuffed with money, the Cyclone had real cars instead of roller-coaster cars on its track, and the Teacups were filled with gold.

L'il Mellem picked up a piggybank. "Piggy go to market," he said.

"You're a piggy," said FiFi.

"No, ***Otooneth*** is," said

Otto. "She brainwashed all these people with her taffy and made them bring her their valuable possessions. Now that they don't have anything left to give her, she doesn't need them anymore."

"But what is she going to do with this

junk?" asked FiFi. "She left it all out in the rain."

"No one can use this much stuff. She just wants it. She's got the worst case of greediness in the history of the world," said Otto.

"Oh yes, Ottie, you've solved the case," said Aunt FooFoo. "Now let's go to sleep. Look what I found."

She had curled up on a cozy sofa in the sand.

Just then, the whiny voice boomed over the megaphone.

"Okay, you thupid, thlacker thtoogeth, line up. Firtht 24 thlugs, thit down."

Otto looked up.

The
Parachute
Jump was
ready to go.
People were load-
ing on to the 12 double
seats that were set to rise
250 feet into the air.
Usually, when they reached
the top, the parachutes that
were attached to them
opened up and the seats
floated down. The only
problem was

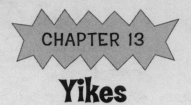

CHAPTER 13

Yikes

these seats had no parachutes!!

CHAPTER 14

Blubberbutts

"Okay, ith everybody ready to fall down and break every bone in their blubber-butts and kick the big ol' bucket?" asked **Otooneth**.

"Yay," shouted the group enthusiastically.

CHAPTER 15

Going Up

Otto steered Racecar into a wheelie.

Half a second later they were at the parachute ride.

The first set of people were almost at the top, kicking their feet and singing "Here Comes the Sun."

"We only have one hope for saving all those people," said Otto. "It's

Yikes Again

Octopus Hands," he gulped.

"Octopoo!" shouted **L'il Mellem**.

"Not *Octopus Hands!*" yelled The Aunts.

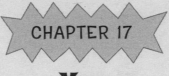

Yup

"Yes, *Octopus Hands*," said Otto.

"Octopoo," said *L'il Mellem*.

"But they're not 100 percent reliable. Can't we use the *Baseball-Glove Roof*?" asked FooFoo.

"It's not big enough," said Otto, steadying his hand on the button.

The seats hit the top of the ride.

"We're out of time. That's it!"

said Otto. He punched the button.

Eight tentacles shot out of Racecar's roof.

The wires holding the seats snapped. The seats tumbled down, wildly, in every direction.

Using the dashboard video screen and

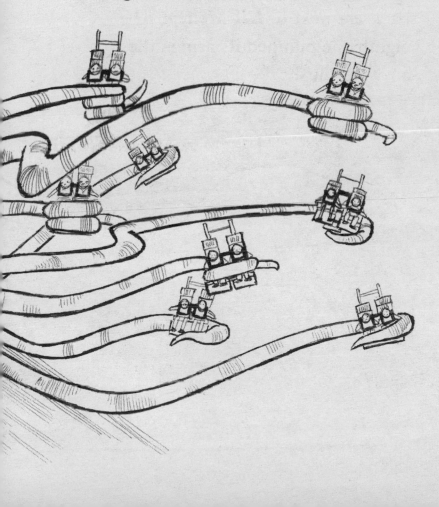

all the physics he had programmed into the device, Otto locked 6 of the 8 heat-seeking tentacles into position to catch the seats.

"Clamp," yelled Otto. The 6 tentacles reached out and caught the 12 falling seats. The seventh tentacle scooped up *Otooneth* and dropped her onto Racecar's backseat next to *L'il Mellem*. The eighth one pumped its arm in the air victoriously.

CHAPTER 18

Oh Susanna

"Let me out of here, you crooked, creepo cabbage headth!" yelled *Otooneth*. Her tissues had fallen out of her nose holes, and she was leaking all over the car.

Otto took out some Silly Putty he kept in the glove compartment.

"Here, Uncle IrfIrf," he said to FiFi, not wanting to touch somebody else's nasal secretions. "Use this to stop the leak."

"Here, FroFro, use this to stop the leak," said FiFi, passing the putty to FooFoo.

"Here, little melon baby, use this to stop the leak," said FooFoo, passing it to *L'il Mellem*.

Mellem put the whole ball of Silly Putty

over **Otooneth**'s nose holes.

"Well done," said Otto.

"How about thome taffy?" said **Otooneth**, holding out a piece of the sparkling candy.

Everyone in the car, except **L'il Mellem**, turned toward it automatically, holding out their hands. It was irresistible.

"Taffy bad," said **L'il Mellem**, and punched **Otooneth** in her tooth. She dropped the candy. FooFoo squashed it with her foot.

CHAPTER 19

Locked Up

They pulled up in front of the taffy shop.

Otto got the collapsible Rolling Prison out of Racecar's trunk.

"Everybody out," he said. "You first, *Otooneth*."

"Don't call me that!" she yelled.

"Isn't that what OS stands for, **Otooneth Snoone**?" asked Otto.

"No, you obnoxiouth object, it thtands for Oh Thuthanna," she said indignantly.

"Band-Aid on a knee," sang *L'il Mellem*, clapping his hands.

FooFoo pushed Oh Susanna into the prison.

Otooneth shrugged her off. "Get your filthy fitht off my fine fabric."

Otto locked the cage.

"Help me roll her into the shop," he said. "We have to find an anti-dote, or these people will be zombies forever."

The crowd was knee dancing and arm flapping behind

the car, soaking wet, still talking about the lovely day.

Otto picked up **L'il Mellem**. "Uncle OrfOrf, come with me. We have work to do in the back. Uncle IrfIrf, you stay up front and guard the prisoner."

"I don't want to," said FiFi. "Get your son to do it."

"He's not my son," said Otto. "Besides, I need someone a few years older, who's

strong and wise and won't fall for any tricks. You're the only person here who fits that description."

FiFi looked around. "You're right. I'll guard her like a chihuahua."

"Thome guard," snickered **Otooneth**. "Chihuahuath are jutht puny, peewee poocheth, who couldn't hurt a hamthter."

FiFi growled and bared her false teeth. **Otooneth** jumped back and banged her head.

Otto, FooFoo, and **L'il Mellem** went into the back of the shop.

CHAPTER 20

Diapers and DNA

"Wow," said Otto. "Look at this place. It's perfect."

It looked like a laboratory from a mad-scientist movie. Different-colored liquids bubbled in beakers of all sizes. Jars of toxic chemicals lined the walls. Glowing strands of taffy were being stretched on huge machines, then moved on a conveyor belt to other machines where they were cut into pieces and wrapped, then dropped into glittering bags.

Otto pulled FooFoo and *L'il Mellem* into a huddle.

"Okay, team, we have to isolate the ingredient in that taffy that's making everyone do whatever *Otooneth* wants them to. Uncle OrfOrf, I need you to use

your cooking skills to figure out exactly what's in the taffy, without touching or tasting it."

"That's not a problem," said FooFoo, rolling up her sleeves. "I have the best sense of smell in the business. I came in first, second, and third in the tongue-tied custard cooking contest 12 years in a row."

"Great," said Otto. He picked up a Q-tip. "*L'il Mellem*, open your mouth, please."

The baby opened his mouth and stuck out his tongue.

"I'm rubbing this cotton swab over the inside of your cheek to get a sample of your DNA," said Otto. "I think that the reason you don't like the taffy is because you are immune to the ingredient that turns everyone else into babbling idiots. I'll analyze your DNA to find the gene that makes you immune. Then maybe I'll be able to make an antidote. I hope."

Otto removed the Q-tip and rubbed the sample onto a microscope slide.

"Okay, I'm going into **DNA land**," he said, taking out the atomic-force microscopic lens he kept in his ring.

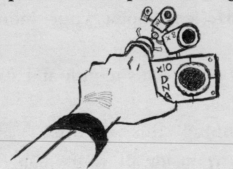

"Wait a minute, I smell the evil ingredient already," said FooFoo. "It's poop!"

"Sorry, Uncle OrfOrf, that's the baby's diaper you're smelling. Would you change it, please?" asked Otto.

"Daddy do it," said *L'il Mellem*.

"He wants you to do it, Ottie," said FooFoo happily.

Otto had no choice. He took the clean diaper off *L'il Mellem*'s head, held his breath, and tried not to look. He gagged and almost passed out, but he changed the diaper. Then he found a sink and washed his hands furiously, using an entire bar of soap.

CHAPTER 21

Guard Duty

Meanwhile, FiFi was still growling at **Otooneth**.

"Thothe bungling boneheadth will never find an antidote," said **Otooneth**. "It took me my whole life to create that candy. I ate nothing but taffy for 20 yearth. How do you think I lotht my teeth?"

"Grrrrrrr," said FiFi.

"Quit growling," said **Otooneth**. "I've been around worth animalth than you. How do you think I lotht my nothe?"

"Grrrrrrr?" asked FiFi, interested.

"A rat mithtook it for a piethe of taffy and bit it off. I thquished him till he thquealed," she continued. "Can't blame him, though, nobody can rethitht my taffy."

"Grrrrrrr," said FiFi fiercely.

"Wanna piethe of taffy?" **Otooneth** asked, suddenly pulling one out of a hidden pocket.

"Yes, please," said FiFi sweetly, holding out her hands.

CHAPTER 22

Taffy Examined

FooFoo was standing at a table blind-folded, with her arms tied behind her back, examining the candy with her nose. But it still took a lot of effort to resist its power.

L'il Mellem was on the floor, playing with the wrapped taffy pieces like they were LEGOs.

"It's amazing," said Otto. "The taffy has no effect on him at all."

"I've got it," declared FooFoo excitedly. "This taffy is full of TX68, the same chemical my great friend, the crazed scientist

Elmo Shlomo, discovered before he died in 1973. At the time he was looking for a cure for indigestion and fatal farting. But before he could test his discovery, he cut the cheese and died. The fart fumes were so powerful that the area was quarantined, and the house burned to the ground along with any record of his work."

"That makes perfect sense," said Otto excitedly. "We now know that TX68 is the main chemical in the 'Follow the Leader' gene. A dose of pure TX68 would overpower all the other genes in a person's DNA. Anyone who eats the taffy will do whatever **Otooneth** says, and merrily."

"Merrily roll along, quack quack duckie poo," sang *L'il Mellem*.

"Look at this!" said Otto, peering intently into the microscope. "*L'il Mellem*'s Follow the Leader gene is a mutation. It has the backward chemical, 86XT, the exact opposite of everyone else's. All we have to do is duplicate the mutation, inject it into some taffy, and we have our antidote!"

CHAPTER 23

Road Trip

FiFi finished the taffy and had two more pieces. She was under its spell.

"Give me thomething, and let me out of here, you cheethey chihuahua," said *Otooneth*.

"I have a lovely present for your beautiful majesty on this clear and sunny day," said FiFi, opening the prison lock.

"Well, what ith it, you putrid puppy?" asked *Otooneth*.

"It's a car," said FiFi, walking her to Taxi-Racecar.

"I have two thouthand carth, and thith ith jutht a thtupid taxi!" said *Otooneth*.

"This one is special,"

said FiFi. She turned Racecar on and pressed the *Mission Car* option. The taxi shell disappeared.

"Hey, not bad for a mangy mutt," said **Otooneth**.

"Bright and sunny," said FiFi. "It goes fast, too, and does tricks. What should I do now?"

"Get in," said **Otooneth**. "I'm thick of Coney Island. Drive me to the White

Houthe. I want to give thome nithe taffy to
the prethident. Then he can go on TV and
tell the American thitizenth to bring me all
their thtuff. And I will
be the richetht
woman in the
world!"

"We'll be there before you can say 'warm
and toasty,'" said FiFi.

She put Racecar into gear and sped off.

CHAPTER 24

Rrrrrm

"Did you hear that?" asked Otto. "It sounded like Racecar."

"Rrrrm, rrrrrm, go fast, beep beep, turkey poo," said *L'il Mellem*.

"Right," said Otto.

"I'll go check," said Aunt FooFoo. She got up quickly and rushed to the door. Too bad, she still had a scarf over her eyes. She smashed into the wall and fell down.

"Boom," said *L'il Mellem*.

Meanwhile, Otto had a really bad feeling. He was out the door in a flash. What he saw made him feel much worse.

CHAPTER 25

What Otto Saw

CHAPTER 26

Anything You Can Do

Otooneth and FiFi were moving fast. At this rate, they would be in Washington, DC, before dawn. Every once in a while, *Otooneth* gave FiFi another piece of taffy. She had a lot of it hidden in her clothing.

"Thith ith boring, and you thmell like thmoked thmelts," said *Otooneth*. "Do thomething to entertain me."

"Yes, Your Marvelous Majesty," said FiFi. She pressed *Voice Command*. "I'll show you some tricks.

"Left Wheel, Rise," she said, then *"Right Wheel, Rise,"* then *"Leap Frog."* Racecar did as he was told.

"What'th tho good about that?" said *Otooneth*. "Anyone can do that. Pull over."

FiFi stopped the car.

"Watch me," said *Otooneth*.
She got out and stood on one
leg and then the other. Then
she started jumping like a
frog.

FiFi clapped her hands.
"Not a cloud in the sky," she
said.

"Can that machine do
thith?" She did a double
somersault.

FiFi made Racccar do
one too.

"Before I wath a taffy
torturer, I wath an actual
amazing agile athlete thpe-
cializing in acrobaticth,"
revealed *Otooneth*. "And
thith ith jutht a corroded
car. I challenge it to a duel
for the championthip."

79

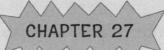

CHAPTER 27

Back at the Shop

"I need a car," yelled Otto, running into the back of the shop. "I need a car to get my car. My car is gone. FiFi is gone. *Otooneth* is gone. They took my car. Racecar is gone."

"What, no hello?" said Aunt FooFoo.

"The remote isn't working. They're too far away. I've got to catch up to them before something terrible happens."

"*Mellem* go car rrrrm rrrrm," said *L'il Mellem*, running around in circles.

"Go car, that's it!" cried Otto. "There are kiddie go-carts right next door. Great idea, *l'il* leader," said Otto.

"*L'il Mellem*," said *Mellem*.

"It'll be risky, but I think it can work," said Otto. "I'll replace the gas in the go-cart with my Quick-as-a-Jick fuel mixture and harness some lunar power. Uncle OrfOrf, you stay here with *L'il Mellem* and keep working on the antidote."

"Me go car, Daddy," said *L'il Mellem*, starting to cry.

"Okay, okay, little guy, you can come," said Otto. He couldn't stand hearing a baby cry. It made him too sad.

"Waaaaaaaa," bawled Aunt FooFoo. "Me come too."

"But I need you to make the antidote," said Otto.

"I already did," said FiFi. "I put in a dash of Imitation Roadrunner, my new secret ingredient for speedy cooking. Here's the first batch of taffy, fresh out of the oven. It's got a little walnut caramel flavoring. Delicious."

"Will it work?" asked Otto.

"I don't know," said FooFoo.

"Taffy good," said *L'il Mellem*.

"Really?" asked Otto.

"Turkey head doggy poo," said *L'il Mellem*.

"Okay, let's all go," said Otto. "Bring the antidote taffy with you. We might need it."

Then he had a thought. He carefully picked up a piece of the bad taffy with some tongs, dropped it into a plastic bag, and sealed it.

They raced out of the shop, past the people doing their knee dance, to the

CHAPTER 28

Operation Rescue

go-cart ride next door.

Otto took one of the little carts and filled the tank with his fuel mixture, which included espresso coffee, Tabasco, and chili pepper oil. Then he unpeeled the top of his driver's helmet, exposing an underlay of convertible solar/lunar panels. Aunt FooFoo did a speedy check of the tires and brakes.

They couldn't all fit in the go-cart's single seat. Luckily, Otto never went anywhere without additional seat belts of all kinds. He told Aunt FooFoo to lie down on the roll bar on top of the car, and he strapped her on securely. Then he hooked himself in and put *L'il Mellem* between his legs, with a helmet and double

strap crisscrossed around his chest.

Otto put up his radar-tracking device, which was on his ring, and locked in to Racecar's signal.

"They seem to be standing still somewhere on the side of the road. Let's hit it," he said.

The rain had stopped. Energy from the full moon surged through the lunar panels in Otto's helmet, into his body, and out his shoe.

He put his foot on the gas pedal, and they took off.

CHAPTER 29

Floor Exercises

"Okay, thith ith my latht trick," said **Otooneth**, pointing at Racecar. "I'm going to win or I'm going to break every bone in thith wobbly wagon's entire engine."

Otooneth took a deep breath, then did a triple cartwheel into a back handstand, twirled around into a double pirouette twist, did a split in the air, and landed on one foot.

This was too much for FiFi to remember.

She got the order mixed up, and Racecar lost the match.

"I win!" exclaimed **Otooneth**. "I'm the betht, the thmartetht, the motht beautiful and the richetht. I'm better than thith broken-down, beaten-up, burnt-out bobthled!" She was delighted.

"Warm and sunny, warm and sunny," said FiFi, clapping her hands. "What should I do now?" she asked.

Otooneth climbed into the back of Racecar. She put a whole box of tissues over her nose holes.

"Drive," she said. "It'th time for my nap. Wake me up when we get to the White Houthe."

CHAPTER 30

Dino-Snorus

Otto was driving like he was in the Indianapolis 500, and the little go-cart was rattling around like Jell-O in a washing machine. The tires were worn to shreds, but Otto wouldn't stop for FooFoo to patch them. She squeezed Otto's Secret Formula Rubber Cement out of a tube and onto the tires while the wheels were still in motion.

L'il Mellem was having a ball.

"Me drive more fast rrrm rrrm," he said, over and over again. "Me push button."

The go-cart went around a bend, and Otto saw Racecar.

"Okay, *Mellem*," he said, "push this button."

L'il Mellem put his hand on the horn.

FiFi looked in the rearview mirror and saw them approaching, but she was deep into her assignment of getting to the White House. She just kept driving.

Otooneth, asleep in the backseat, was snoring. If you never heard a person with no nose snore, it's kind of like an angry

Tyrannosaurus rex with a head cold. Only worse.

FiFi loved it. She started singing along to the snoring in the note of A-flat.

Bright and sun - ny Warm and toast - y

Not a cloud in the sky

No pre - cip - i - ta - tion

Winds out of the west

Ba - rom - e - ter low

Ze - ro hu - mid - i - ty

Ee - yi Ee - yi o

CHAPTER 31

Back and Forth

Racecar was in range. Otto pulled out his remote control and said, *"Reverse."*

Racecar backed up toward Otto.

But FiFi switched Racecar to *Manual Override* and said, *"Forward."*

Racecar went forward again.

"Remote Mode—Reverse," said Otto.

The car went backward.

"Manual Override—Forward," said FiFi. Racecar went forward.

Otto tried, *"Remote Mode—About Face."* Racecar turned around, and started coming toward him.

FiFi said, *"Manual Override—About Face."* The car turned around and started going forward again.

Racecar was going in circles. Otto figured if he could just keep this up for a couple of minutes, he would overtake FiFi and **Otooneth**.

But FiFi was a master mechanic, and she had a mission. She disconnected the remote control fuse. FiFi put her foot on the gas and Racecar sped away.

CHAPTER 32

Still Born to Drive

There was no way the little go-cart could match the speed of Racecar. This situation called for some wild driving.

Otto needed an idea. His best ideas usually came when someone held a lightbulb over his head.

Just then the first ray of morning sunlight came up and hit the solar panel on Otto's helmet. It was a million times as bright as a bulb.

Otto spied a diner with a sloped roof on the side of the road. Beside it was a broken-up parking lot with a towering mound of dirt. He did some rapid-fire calculations.

If he drove up the dirt mound really fast, he could make the go-cart leap onto the roof and, from there, launch the cart into the air and fly above the road. The winds were gusting in just the right direction to push him forward. If he steered correctly and made an ace landing, he might be able to get ahead of Racecar.

"Hang on, guys, we're going off-road," said Otto. "OrfOrf, give it some juice."

"Got it!" cried FooFoo. She added a dash of Imitation Roadrunner to the fuel tank.

The go-cart took off like a rocket. Otto veered sharply to the right, steered into the lot, and hit the mound of dirt hard and fast. The go-cart

landed on the roof of the diner, front wheels in the air.

Otto hunkered down for the launch, but **L'il Mellem** put his hands on the steering wheel and screamed, "*Mellem* drive!" Startled, Otto released his grip only for a split second, but that was enough to send them off course. They went careening onto the top of a tall thin tree. The tree bent way back, then swung forward, pitching the go-cart up and over into the air.

"*Mellem* fly," said *L'il Mellem*.

FooFoo screamed.

Otto looked at the road down below. Racecar was zooming forward.

"Put out your arms," he yelled to FooFoo. She did.

He drove the little car like a glider by jerking the steering wheel and leaning hard to the left, then hard to the right, using FooFoo's arms as wings. They landed right beside Racecar, sparks flying from what was left of the tires.

Now the two cars were even and coasting along at the same speed.

Otto could see FiFi through Racecar's open window.

She was still singing her heart out.

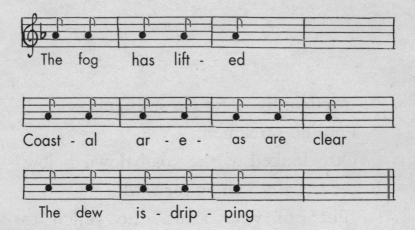

The fog has lift - ed

Coast - al ar - e - as are clear

The dew is - drip - ping

Otto had to take a big chance. It was the only way.

"Okay, *Mellem*, drive now!" said Otto, putting the toddler's hands on the wheel.

CHAPTER 33

The Big Chance

Otto got out a slingshot and loaded it with the taffy that had the antidote.

"Uncle IrfIrf, taffy!" called Otto. She turned her head. He shot the candy. The taffy landed in her mouth. Bull's-eye!

The antidote took effect immediately.

"Grrrrr," said FiFi, coming out of her trance.

Otto got out Racecar's remote control,

and took back the go-cart steering wheel.

"Good job, *L'il Mellem*. Now push this button," said Otto.

"*Mellem* push," he said, punching the **Park** button on Racecar's remote.

Now Otto had to stop the go-cart. He put his foot on the brake, but nothing happened. The go-cart was falling apart. Suddenly all four tires blew out. The naked wheels hit the ground and flew off. Skidding on its belly, the go-cart headed toward a cement wall. Aunt FooFoo howled with terror.

Otto checked their position on his ring tracking device.

"Impact minus 22.76 yards," he shouted, giving their exact position.

"One, two, buckle my shoe," said *Mellem*.

"Octopus Hands," screamed Otto into the remote.

"Octopoo," said **Mellem**.

An instant later, only inches from crashing into the wall, the go-cart was snatched into the air by the *Octopus Hands* and plunked down safely on the side of the road, right next to Racecar.

CHAPTER 34

Otooneth Tamed

Otto unstrapped himself, then *L'il Mellem* and FooFoo.

FiFi was growling at ***Otooneth***, who was still fast asleep. She was roaring with snoring, bubbling mucus erupting in rivers out of her nose holes and running everywhere. There was ***tons o' snot***.

Otto took out the slingshot with ***Otooneth***'s taffy and aimed it at her open mouth.

"***Mellem*** do it," said ***L'il Mellem***.

"We'll do it together," said Otto. They pulled back the slingshot and launched the taffy into her mouth.

Otooneth woke up, choking. FooFoo thought she was going to have to give her the Heimlich maneuver. But then Miss O

Tons o' snot is a palindrome.

swallowed the taffy.

Her eyes went blank. She smiled. She sat up, flapped her arms, and lifted her knees.

"What a thunthiny day," she said. "A wonderouth warm dathling dainty day. Not a cumulouth cloud in the thky. What thould I do now?"

Otto drove Racecar straight to a U-Wash-Car place and handed her a rag and a hose. *Otooneth* happily scrubbed Racecar till he twinkled like a pile of taffy.

CHAPTER 35

Gnarly

When they got back to Coney Island, it really was a bright sunny day. The taffy zombies were still doing their knee-jerking dance and flapping their arms, calling for taffy. They must have been pretty tired.

Otto ran into the back of the shop and phoned the police. The Aunts got all the antidote taffy off the conveyor belt. Just to be safe, Otto and FooFoo had one each, then passed the rest out to the crowd. They gave *Otooneth* an extra dose of her own candy.

As soon as the zombies chewed their taffy, they fell to the ground, dazed and exhausted, but at least they were no longer under *Otooneth*'s power.

Otto got the megaphone and made an

announcement explaining to them what had happened. Then he said, "And now a word from Oh Susanna, who wants to say something before she spends the rest of her life in prison." He handed her the bullhorn.

"Nithe day, ithn't it?" said **Otooneth**. "Warm and toathty. Bright and thiny. What thould I do now?"

"Apologize and give them their stuff back," said Otto.

"I'm thorry, and you can have your thtuff back at onthe." She walked through the crowd handing back the

105

things she was wearing.

"This thaffire ith for you, and thethe gold goodieth are for you," she said as she went along.

"The retht of your thtuff ith on the beach," she said merrily. "You thould altho check the rideth. I put a lot of thingth there."

One youngish man got up from his stupor. He had long dark hair streaked with red and purple. He came barreling over to *Otooneth*. He was plenty mad.

"Where did you put my

exceptional little boy baby, you nasty witch?" he said.

"Big Daddy," said *L'il Mellem*, jumping into his arms and pulling his hair.

"Little Melvin, dude!" said the man, hugging *Mellem* tight.

"Oh, your name is Melvin," said Otto.

"L'il Mellem," agreed Melvin.

"Yeah, that's what we call him. Hey, and that's my way cool jacket with like the shiny studs all over it," said the dad.

"Here you are," said *Otooneth* pleasantly, taking it off.

"Now it's got your gnarly cooties all over it. Bummer!" said the dad, shaking the jacket.

Otto wanted to tell Melvin's dad how special his son was. He wanted to invite them over to his house and play with *L'il Mellem* and teach him how to drive. He wanted *L'il Mellem* to be his little brother. But he couldn't do any of those things, because he was an undercover agent, and he was going to have to disappear before he and The Aunts and Racecar were discovered for who they really were.

Otto saw the police pull up and knew that his work here was done. "C'mon, Uncles, let's go," said Otto. They got into Racecar and drove off.

CHAPTER 36

Crystal Love

Once again, Otto was left with that empty feeling he had after every mission. He was especially sad this time because he was never going to see *L'il Mellem* again.

Suddenly, there was a sonic boom. Then it began to hail. Ice crystals fell onto Racecar's windshield.

"What's with the weather in this place anyway?" asked Otto.

A second later, the hail stopped and the crystals melted. There was a message on Racecar's windshield, written in water stains. It said:

DEAR JAKE, OUR WONDERFUL SON, WHO WE LOVE MORE THAN EVERY UNIVERSE EVER DISCOVERED OR IMAGINED

ANOTHER BRILLIANT
MISSION COMPLETED!
THE COUNTRY IS SAFE AND
IT'S BECAUSE OF YOU.
DON'T GO HOME YET!
CONEY ISLAND IS AN AMUSEMENT
PARK, AND YOU'RE A LITTLE BOY.
STAY HERE AND GOOF AROUND!

REMEMBER, WE ARE ALWAYS WITH
YOU EVEN THOUGH WE'RE IN A PLANE
MOVING SEVEN TIMES THE SPEED
OF SOUND, HOT ON THE TRAIL OF
THE TALL SKINNY MAN WITH THE
LONG DANGLING HEAD.

PLEASE WASH THIS MESSAGE OFF.
THE FLOPPY-HEAD GUY CAN READ.

LOVE, MOM AND DAD

Happily, Otto turned on the water
sprayers and washed off the message with
his windshield wipers.

Just then a street-cleaner truck passed
by, rudely spraying water all over Racecar's
window. But the water dried instantly,

leaving a second message:

P.S. CYCLE ON
AND CUT PEAS.

Otto got that one right away. It was time to have some fun.

"Okay, men," he said, "it's time to put your *moustaches* back in their *mouth cases*."

"No rest today again?" asked FooFoo.

"Nope," said Otto. "The day before *yesterday* was the *day ye rest*, and maybe tomorrow, but I'm not promising."

111

CHAPTER 37

Dude

Otto and The Uncles changed back into Otto and The Aunts.

Mission Car morphed back into Racecar.

The man who was operating the Cyclone recognized Racecar because he was one of the most famous cars in America. He proudly guarded the car while Otto went on the roller coaster 25 times. The Aunts went on the Teacups. They were so dizzy from going around 30 times that they forgot to get off.

Otto picked them up, but even when they were back on their feet, they just kept spinning. Otto knew that the best cure for severe dizziness was cotton candy, so they stumbled over to the nearest stand.

That's where they bumped into *L'il Mellem* and his dad.

Melvin recognized Otto right away. Melvin's dad didn't, because even though he was pretty young, he was still a grown-up and most grown-ups can't tell one kid from another.

"*L'il* Daddy," said Melvin.

"Sorry, dude," said the dad. "He was

calling this other kid daddy before too. I guess it's a stage."

"I'm Otto Pillip," said Otto.

"Whoa," said Melvin's dad. "You're that small racecar driver dude. No way!"

"Way," said Otto, "and these spinning ladies are my aunts."

"I'm *Donod*," said Melvin's dad.

"Donald?" asked Otto.

"Yeah, well, it was Donald, but I changed it to *Donod*. It's way cooler."

"Way," said Otto.

"Way, way," said *Donod*.

Just then *Donod*'s cell phone rang.

Donod is a palindrome.

114

CHAPTER 38

Opportunity Poo

"Yo," answered **Donod**. "Oh no, dude . . .
no . . . dude . . . no, dude . . . no,
dude . . . oh dude . . . no, dude.
Dude." He hung up.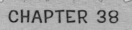

"Bad news?" asked Otto.

"Dude," said **Donod**.
"The lead singer and gui-
tar player in my band
has some kind of rare
virus. The symptoms are gurgle voice and
finger rot. We're playing at the Off Key
tonight and he has a 112-degree fever."

"You're in a band?" asked Otto.

"Yeah, dude, we're called the Steaming
Oranges."

"No way," said Otto.

"Way," said Melvin's dad.

"I may be able to help you," said Otto. Besides wanting to see his parents again, he wanted to be in a band more than anything in the world. "I'm a pretty good guitar player myself."

"No way," said *Donod*.

"Way, way," said Otto.

"But you don't know any of our tunes," said *Donod*.

"That's true, but I've got some amazing songs of my own. If you lend me a guitar and I play lead, maybe you guys could back me up," offered Otto.

"Would you do that, dude?" asked *Donod*.

"For sure," said Otto.

"Turtle head horsey poo," said *L'il Mellem*.

"Cool," said *Donod*. "We go on at eight."

CHAPTER 39

Rock Show

That night Otto and The Aunts showed up at the Off Key. It was jammed. *Donod* and Melvin met them at the door.

"My aunt FiFi sings backup and tap dances," said Otto.

"Cool," said *Donod*. "*Pat and Edna tap* too." Pat and Edna were the band's groupies.

"My aunt FooFoo cooks," said Otto.

"I need to cook," said FooFoo. She was looking a little twitchy.

"Exceptional," said *Donod*. "I need to eat."

They went inside to set up. FooFoo went straight to the kitchen.

The show was actually pretty bad. Otto sang vocals and played guitar, *Donod* drowned him out on the drums,

Pat and Edna tap is a palindrome.

118